CW01583504

Dedicated to my nephews and nieces who
inspire me every time we meet.

Eimaan, Yahya, Dawood,
Mishal and Ishaaq,
Thank you so much.

Dear Zakariya,

I hope you enjoy the Story.
Never give up on your dreams
or ambitions.

Happy reading.
Best Wishes
Aisha.
10 Jul 2016

Two little fox cubs returned home one afternoon,
from a wander in the woods
as it would be tea time soon.

As they passed a rickety house deep in the woods,
they huddled close together and walked as fast as they could.
"Do you know who lives there?"
said Foxy Foo's big brother.
"A horrible old lady who once tried to catch Mother."

Foxy Foo's eyes were wide with fright.
He tried to stop shaking with all his might.
"She kidnaps foxes and takes off their tail,
uses them for handbags and puts them on sale."
Both the cubs ran through the bushes and trees,
reaching the den, ... shaking to their knees.

An old woman watched as quiet as a mouse,
as two little fox cubs ran past the house.

The next day Foxy Foo's brother was too ill to play,
he had a fever, so indoors he would have to stay.
By 11 o' clock Foxy Foo was bored,
staying indoors was such a chore.
"Mother may I please go to Joey's house to play?
He's always said I can come over any time of day."
"Of course my dear," his mother said happily.
"But just make sure you're home, in time for tea."

Foxy Foo started off through the woods,
it would take 20 minutes if his pace was good.
He hopped and skipped among the trees,
nearly upsetting a hive of bees.

The little cub came to a fork in the road,
not knowing which way he should go.
"Hmmm," he thought, "Right or left, which way will be best?"
Foxy Foo picked the path on the right,
as it looked correct and it looked bright.

After a while the path began to look strange,
but Foxy Foo continued just the same.
He hadn't realised but he'd passed through a gate,
and now we can only guess his fate.

A few moments later he looked on in alarm,
at the rickety house that stood next to a barn.
Foxy Foo couldn't believe his sight,
he turned and ran so fast, he almost took flight.

At the gate stood the old woman, with hair that was grey.
Was Foxy Foo her latest prey?

He didn't see her until it was too late,
the old woman had already closed the gate!

She walked towards him with a fixed gaze,
for Foxy Foo it was all a haze.
His head began to spin and his body sway,
was it really going to end this way?
The old woman bent down and picked him up, ...

... took him inside and placed him next to a very big cup.
"Now little one, since you're here with me,
I think we should have some tea."

Foxy Foo slowly opened his eyes,
at what he saw he was completely surprised.
The old lady was singing and dancing,
around the kitchen she was shockingly prancing.

"I am so happy to have a guest,
I will serve you the very best."
The old woman prepared the biscuits and cakes,
and in front of Foxy Foo placed the most beautiful plate.

Foxy Foo didn't eat from the platter.
He thought the old woman was trying to make him fatter.
He'd heard a story a long time ago,
so he thought he was already in the know.
"What's wrong little foxy, why don't you eat?
I thought all this would be a wonderful treat."

She sat back and looked rather sad,
Foxy Foo felt a little bit bad.
Maybe the stories about the old woman were wrong,
maybe she wasn't scary all along.
"You're free to go anytime you wish.
I meant you no harm I sincerely promise.
I get so lonely and upset,
being all alone makes me fret ...

I just wanted some company as you can see,
it's been years since someone has come round for tea.
There had been another fox who had come this way,
she was so frightened by me,
I accidently scared her away."

Foxy Foo looked at the old lady
and a smile materialised,
it had all been a big misunderstanding
both of them realised.

After finishing the cake and enjoying a chat,
Foxy Foo ran home more swiftly than a cat.

Since that day Foxy Foo and his family
regularly visit that house
and they no longer have to be as quiet as a mouse.

THE END

ISBN 978-0-9928533-7-2

Cover Design: Bookcraft Ltd

Printed by Lightning Source

Published by:
PERFECT PUBLISHERS LTD
23 Maitland Avenue
Cambridge
CB4 1TA
England

http://www.perfectpublishers.co.uk

Perfect Publishers Ltd

Lightning Source UK Ltd.
Milton Keynes UK
UKOW07f1825290616

277244UK00001B/4/P